MHH

LEO THE LOP
TAIL ONE

Written by Stephen Cosgrove
Illustrated by Robin James

A Serendipity™ *Book*

W9-AZC-181

PSS!
PRICE STERN SLOAN

The Serendipity™ Series was created by Stephen Cosgrove and Robin James.

Copyright © 2002, 1978 by Price Stern Sloan. All rights reserved.
Published by Price Stern Sloan, a division of
Penguin Young Readers Group, 345 Hudson Street, New York, New York 10014.

Library of Congress Catalog Card Number: 94-21148

ISBN 978-0-8431-7723-7

Revised Edition

2010 Printing

Dedicated to Wendy James, then and now,
and to the memory of
the one and only Leo the Lop.
—Stephen

Beyond the horizon, farther than far, in the middle of the Crystal Sea, was a beautiful island called Serendipity. On this magical island, in the middle of the Forest of Dreams, protected by a wall of flowers and ferns was a wonderful place called the Thicket. It was in the Thicket that the Serendipity bunnies lived.

Here bunnies of every shade of fur lived and played their lives away; there were white ones, brown ones, some with spots, and one even dappled in dots.

As much as they seemed different the bunnies were all the same—each had a cute little nose, a fluffy puff of a tail, and two perky ears that stood straight up in the air.

All of them, that is, save for Leo the Lop.

Now it wasn't that Leo didn't have a cute little nose or a fluffy puff of a tail, for he did. What made him so different was that he didn't have ears that stood straight up. Instead his ears hung straight down.

Ears were of little importance to Leo because he thought himself just as normal as could be.

Day by day, as the little bunnies grew older, they began to notice that Leo was a little different. The more they looked at him the more the difference seemed to grow bigger and bigger.

And to the other little bunnies the difference seemed very funny, indeed.

Whenever Leo hopped by on the Twisty Trail that spiraled through the Forest of Dreams, the other bunnies would grab their sides and giggle and laugh. They weren't trying to be mean and they really didn't want to hurt Leo's feelings, but they just couldn't stop themselves from laughing.

You must admit that a bunny hopping about with his ears dragging behind, is a pretty funny sight.

Leo was confused by the laughter. He didn't see anything funny about the way he looked. His fur was the same as the other rabbits. His tail was the same as the other rabbits. As far as Leo could tell he was just as normal as normal could be.

Finally in frustration he muttered, "Hey! How come you guys are always laughing at me?"

"It's your ears," giggled Buttermilk. "They go down, not up. You aren't normal." With that, she and the others hopped into the forest, their laughter echoing behind.

Leo felt kind of bad. He didn't think any differently than the other rabbits, but it seemed because he looked different, he was different. Therefore he must not be normal.

"This being 'not normal' can't be a forever thing," muttered Leo. "All I need to do is exercise a bit, and my ears will stand up straight just like the normal bunnies' ears. Then they won't have anything to laugh about." So, he clenched his furry fists, scrunched his eyes really tight and grunted and groaned with all of his might, trying desperately to get his ears to stand up.

Unfortunately, the best he could do was to get them to stick straight out; hardly a normal rabbit kind of thing.

But Leo the Lop was not one to give up easily. Surely there were other ways to make his ears appear to be normal.

"Maybe I just need to show my ears the way to go, and then they will know what to do."

Very carefully he climbed up into the old twisted possum tree that stood near the middle of the Thicket, hooked his hind legs over the branch, and then dangled over hanging upside down.

Sure enough his ears hung straight up, or rather straight down from his head. Leo the Lop looked just as normal as normal could be. . .

. . .or did he?

As the story goes, Leo hung there for an hour more, swinging gently in the breeze as his ears learned to hang up instead of down.

He would have hung there even longer, but he was startled nearly out of his wits as someone called out in a long slow drawl, "Whatcha doin'?"

Leo turned his head, and there, hanging right beside him was the possum who lived in the old possum tree.

"Uh, well," said Leo as he scratched his cheek, "I'm hanging upside down so my ears will learn to stick straight up. When my ears stand up I can be a normal rabbit."

"Hmm," wondered the possum. "What is normal? When I saw you on the ground, your ears looked normal to me. Now they look upside down."

Leo thought and thought, and you know, he didn't really know *what* normal was.

With a flip Leo the Lop flopped to the ground, the possum's question ringing in his ears.

"If my ears drooping down are normal," he thought, "then the other rabbits' ears going up must not be normal at all."

He thought about it and he thought about it and the more he thought about it the funnier the thought became. He was normal; they were not.

With his heart full of laughter he hopped off to the others to tell them his good news.

Giggling, Leo told the other rabbits what he had been told by the possum from the possum tree.

If the truth be known, the other bunnies didn't know whether to believe him or not. As Leo laughed and laughed, they thought about it, and the more they thought about it, the more it made sense. Their ears went up not down. They were not normal.

"What are we to do?" they whined.

"I've an idea," said Buttermilk brightly. "We'll teach our ears to go down, not up!" She found two large stones and with a bit of wild twine-vine she tied the stones to the tops of her ears. With the weight of the stones her ears began to droop lower and lower until they were touching the ground.

Excited at Buttermilk's success in making herself appear normal, the others rushed about picking up stones and gathering lengths of vine.

Everything would have been perfectly perfect in the Thicket except for one itty-bitty problem—the rocks and ears became tangled in feet and tails. Bunnies tripped and plopped into one big furry pile.

"Very funny, bunnies," they grumbled as one. "This is not going to work!"

"Well," said Buttermilk as she untied the twine-vine from the stones, "maybe we need to show our ears the way to go, and then they will know what to do. Then we will be just as normal as Leo."

Together the five little rabbits climbed up into the old possum tree. With the twine-vine they tied their ears to the branch, they flipped over and hung upside down.

Sure enough their ears hung straight down, or rather straight up toward the branch. All the rabbits looked just as normal as normal could be. . .or did they?

As the story goes, they hung there for an hour more, swinging gently in the breeze as their ears learned to hang down instead of up.

They would have hung there even longer, but they were startled as someone called out in a long slow drawl, "Whatcha doin'?"

Scared nearly out of their wits, they quickly flopped to the ground and would have run away had they not seen the possum hanging by his tail.

"Well," said Buttermilk defensively as the others gathered around, "we were hanging from the branch so that our ears would be normal like Leo's."

"Hmm," drawled the possum, "what is normal?" He slowly scratched his head and said, "Earlier when I saw you all on the ground, your ears looked very normal. But a moment ago, when you were hanging in the tree, they didn't look normal at all. Truly, they looked as abnormal as could be."

The rabbits stood about thinking deeply about what the possum had said. It was Buttermilk who brightly said, "If we're normal and Leo is normal, then normal is whatever you are!"

Excited they rushed off to find Leo and tell him what they had discovered.

Buttermilk told Leo what the possum had taught them. It made so much sense that Leo easily and happily agreed.

"Normal is whatever I am, and whoever you are!" he laughed.

From that day forward, all of the rabbits lived wonderfully normal lives on the Island of Serendipity.

IF YOU WORRY HOW YOU LOOK

AND THINGS YOU WISH TO SWAP

REMEMBER A NORMAL-EARED RABBIT

DELIGHTFULLY CALLED LEO THE LOP

All was fine on the Island of Serendipity,
although Leo had one tiny, little problem. . .

. . . Leo's ears still drooped in his soup!

Serendipity™ *Books*

Created by
Stephen Cosgrove and Robin James

Enjoy all the delightful books in the Serendipity™ Series:

Available wherever books are sold.

PSS!
PRICE STERN SLOAN

A Serendipity™ Book

Serendipity™ books have warmed the hearts of young and old for over two decades, becoming classics in children's literature.

Each beloved tale teaches youngsters how to deal with the challenges of their world, providing them with positive solutions to difficult problems.

Join the whimsical characters in this beautifully illustrated collection as they entertain and inspire every reader.

PSS!
PRICE STERN SLOAN

ISBN 978-0-8431-7723-7

EAN

9 780843 177237

5 0 4 9 9>

$4.99 US
($7.50 CAN

Pressing
RESET
— for the —
Everyday
Person

⏻riginal
strength